Disney's
Two-Minute
Good Night Stories

By MARY PACKARD

Illustrated by BILL LANGLEY, DIANA WAKEMAN, and PATRICIA KEPPLER

A GOLDEN BOOK • NEW YORK

Western Publishing Company, Inc., Racine, Wisconsin 53404

Scamp the Watchdog

Scamp and his sisters were in the garden one morning.

"Play tag with us, Scamp," said one sister.

But Scamp was thinking about more serious matters.

"I think I'll be a watchdog when I grow up," he said thoughtfully, ignoring his sisters.

"That would be so boring!" said one sister.

Then another sister started to laugh. "Okay, Scamp, be a watchdog right now. Watch us have fun!" And off they ran to play.

"They're such babies!" thought Scamp. "All they ever do is play. A watchdog must be brave and strong, like I am.

"And a watchdog must have great patience and dignity," Scamp continued. "Why, I can just see myself now. I'll start out by guarding a store or a bank. Then I'll work myself up to the Statue of Liberty or maybe even the White House. Of course, I'll win lots of medals for bravery."

Then Scamp heard his mother calling. "Come on, you frisky little puppies!" Lady called. "Lunch is ready!"

"Puppies! Ha!" grumbled Scamp.

After lunch Scamp stood at attention at the front door.

"Are you going out to play, dear?" asked Lady.

"I can't, Mom," said Scamp. "I have to guard the house."

"That's a cute game," said Lady. "Have fun."

"This isn't fun," muttered Scamp. "It's hard work!"

After a while Daniel the mail carrier walked up to the house. Scamp began growling at him, and Daniel slowly backed away.

Lady came running to the door. "What is going on?" she asked.

"Get behind me, Mom," said Scamp. "I'll protect you."

"Don't be silly, Scamp," scolded Lady. "You know Daniel would never hurt us. You ought to be ashamed of yourself!"

"You can't be too careful, Mom," said Scamp. "A watchdog must always be on guard!"

That night at bedtime Scamp's sisters complained about their brother. "Scamp's no fun anymore," they said.

"I'm worried about him, too," said Lady.

"He'll come around," said Tramp. "Just give him some time."

The next day Lady and Tramp invited all their friends to a birthday party for Scamp and his sisters. Only Scamp didn't join the party. He kept watch at the door, growling at each of the guests.

Scamp could hear all the party noises. It sounded as if everyone was having a wonderful time. He felt very lonely. "Maybe being a watchdog isn't such a good idea after all," Scamp thought.

"I think everyone is here, Scamp," said Lady. "Won't you come join the party now?"

"OK, Mom," said Scamp, looking somewhat relieved. "I've decided against being a watchdog anyway. I think I'll be a sheepdog instead. Or maybe a police dog," he continued. "Or even a guide dog…"

Lady laughed at Scamp. "Today I want you to concentrate on being a birthday dog," she said. And she and Scamp ran off to join the party.

Donald Gets Spooked

It was a spooky Halloween night. Donald was home alone, filling bags of candy to give to trick-or-treaters.

Soon the doorbell rang. There before him stood Chip and Dale, who had powdered their fur to make themselves look like mice.

"Oh, no!" said Donald. "I'd know you two troublemakers anywhere. Don't expect any treats from me!" And he chased them off the porch with a broom.

"Of all the nerve!" said Chip.

"He can't treat us like that!" said Dale.

Chip and Dale looked at each other. The same thought popped into their heads. "Let's scare Donald!" they said.

Chip and Dale filled a sack with acorns. Then they climbed up their tree.

"We'll throw these onto Donald's roof," said Dale. "I'll give a loud cackle, and he'll think there's a witch up here."

When the acorns were gone, Chip said, "I have an idea. Follow me!" They scurried down the tree and crawled under the house.

"Tap your paws on the floorboards," said Chip.

"That sure sounds scary!" said Dale. "But I know something even scarier!"

BANG! BANG!

Chip and Dale scampered up a tree and onto the roof. "Ooooooh, oooooooh," they howled into the chimney.

"When Donald hears this, he'll think we're ghosts!" Dale whispered to Chip.

Donald came running out of his house. "Help! Help!" He ran right into Mickey. "My house is haunted!" Donald screamed.

"Calm down," Mickey said. "It's just your imagination."

Chip and Dale were laughing so hard, they nearly fell out of their tree. Since Donald hadn't given them any treats, they had played a trick on him. "That will teach him a lesson!" Chip said to Dale.

Then off Chip and Dale went to find some more Halloween fun.

Grumpy Learns a Lesson

Snow White was in the kitchen when she heard a loud voice from upstairs.

"Why do I always have to go last?"

It was Grumpy again! It seemed that no matter what side of the bed he got up on lately, it was the wrong side.

Before long the Seven Dwarfs were all seated around the table, ready to have breakfast. Snow White took special care in preparing Grumpy's plate. She gave him extra eggs, bacon, and toast. But as soon as she set his plate down, Grumpy said, "Scrambled eggs again? And why don't we ever have sausage? I'm tired of bacon."

The other dwarfs looked at each other. "Looks like it's going to be one of Grumpy's bad days again," whispered Bashful.

After breakfast the Seven Dwarfs started out for work.

"Why do I always have to carry the heaviest shovel?" Grumpy complained.

"It wouldn't be so heavy if you carried it with both hands," said Happy.

"That's the most ridiculous thing I ever heard," said Grumpy. "I'm working by myself today," he added. "That way there won't be anyone to bother me."

The other dwarfs found a spot in the mine where they could all work together.

"I wonder what's wrong with Grumpy," said Sleepy, yawning. "He's grumpier than ever."

"I have an idea," said Doc. "Let's give Grumpy a taste of his own medicine."

Meanwhile, Grumpy worked alone in a different part of the mine. Suddenly he heard the other dwarfs shouting. "I wonder what's going on," he said.

Grumpy went to join the other dwarfs. There he saw them all arguing loudly.

"It's your turn to dig!" Doc yelled at Sleepy.

"Stop bumping me!" Happy shouted at Dopey.

Grumpy couldn't believe his ears. "Hey, what's the matter?" he asked.

"Oh, be quiet!" the other dwarfs said in unison.

Although Grumpy tried to stop them, the other dwarfs complained loudly all the way home. When Snow White heard them, she realized at once that they were trying to teach Grumpy a lesson.

"It's not very nice when people complain and argue," Snow White said to Grumpy.

"Boy, you can say that again!" Grumpy agreed.

The other dwarfs looked at Grumpy. Suddenly Grumpy realized why they had been behaving so badly.

"I guess I have been pretty grumpy," he said in an embarrassed voice. "I'm sorry I got so carried away."

"We forgive you, Grumpy," said the other dwarfs.

"Now let's eat dinner," said Grumpy. "And I'd like to help you get everything ready," he told Snow White with a smile.

Goofy Joins the Band

One day Mickey Mouse and Donald Duck took their nephews to a rock concert.

"Wasn't that a great concert, Uncle Mickey?" asked Ferdie.

"They have a good sound," said Mickey, rubbing his ears, "but don't you think they were a little too loud?"

"No!" said Huey. "They were perfect!"

"I can't wait to get home and start practicing," said Dewey.

"We're going to start our own rock group," said Morty.

Donald and Mickey looked at each other in alarm. "What are you going to call yourselves," asked Donald, "The Noisy Nephews?"

"That's a great name!" the nephews cried.

The next day Morty, Ferdie, Huey, Dewey, and Louie gathered in Donald's basement. They set up their equipment and started rehearsing.

Just then Goofy rang the bell. Donald came to the door wearing earplugs. "The boys have started a rock band," he explained to Goofy.

Goofy couldn't wait to check them out. "Gawrsh!" he said. "You guys sound great! I'm not a nephew, but could I join your band?"

"Well, uh..." said Morty. "Can you play any instruments?"

"Sure!" said Goofy.

Ferdie handed Goofy a guitar. It didn't take more that a few strums for the nephews to decide that the guitar wasn't the best instrument for Goofy.

"Maybe I could sing instead," said Goofy.

Goofy was even worse as a singer. After a minute Huey whispered, "Do you think we could borrow Uncle Donald's earplugs?"

A few days later The Noisy Nephews were ready to put on their first show. They still weren't quite sure what to do with Goofy. But as they began their last rehearsal, Goofy kept time to the music on a bongo drum.

"Hey! Do that again," said Morty.

Goofy tapped on the bongo drum again.

"That's not bad!" cried Dewey.

Before long Mickey, Minnie, Daisy, Donald, and the rest of the audience had arrived. The Noisy Nephews played all their songs perfectly.

"Hey, you guys sound great!" said Mickey.

"I knew they would," said Donald. "After all, they're our nephews."

"And don't forget our star bongo player—Goofy!" said Louie happily.

Buried Treasure

It was a beautiful sunny day. Donald Duck was at the beach with his nephews and Goofy.

"Why don't you build a sand castle while I take a nap," said Donald. "This looks like a good spot."

"That sounds like fun," said Huey.

The castle was coming along nicely when Goofy's shovel hit something hard.

"Gawrsh, what's that?" Goofy asked.

"It looks like some sort of chest," said Louie.

"I bet it's a pirate chest!" cried Dewey. "Let's see what's inside."

Goofy opened the chest. There was a piece of paper inside.

"It says here," said Goofy, "to take thirty paces due south."

Everyone followed Goofy. "Now it says to take fifty paces west to the driftwood," continued Goofy.

They found the driftwood. "Now we take five paces north and dig," Goofy said.

"I bet we'll find a chest full of jewels," said Dewey.

"Or gold!" said Louie.

"Here it is!" cried Huey, pulling a metal chest out of the sand.

"Open it!" said Goofy.

Huey lifted the lid and they all looked inside. "What kind of pirate treasure is that?" asked Dewey.

"It looks pretty valuable to me," said Donald with a chuckle.

"It's our lunch," said Louie with a puzzled look on his face.

Huey finally got the joke. "You really fooled us this time, Uncle Donald!" he said.

"This is the most exciting lunch we ever dug up, though," said Goofy. And they all had a good laugh.

A Surprise for Uncle Scrooge

"Tomorrow is Uncle Scrooge's birthday," said Donald Duck to Mickey Mouse.

"I know," said Mickey, "and I've been thinking. What if we give him a surprise party at his place? All we have to do is get him out of the house so we can get everything ready."

"Great idea," said Donald. "He'll think we forgot about his birthday and he'll really be surprised."

The next morning Mickey, Donald, Huey, Dewey, and Louie drove to Uncle Scrooge's house. They knocked on the door.

"Hi, Uncle Scrooge," said Donald.

"We just came for a visit," said Mickey. "Aren't you going to invite us in?"

"Suit yourselves," said Uncle Scrooge. "But I don't have anything to offer you, since I didn't know you were coming."

Huey, Dewey, and Louie began to pester Uncle Scrooge. "Could you take us to the playground?" asked Louie.

"Absolutely not," said Uncle Scrooge. "It's too noisy there."

"Why don't we go to the park?" asked Dewey.

"That's boring," said Uncle Scrooge.

"How about fishing, Uncle Scrooge?" said Huey. "We know you love to fish."

"Oh, all right," said Uncle Scrooge. "It looks like that's the only way I'll ever get any peace."

After the boys and Uncle Scrooge left, Donald and Mickey baked a birthday cake. They hung up decorations and set the table with party favors. Soon the other guests arrived. When they heard Uncle Scrooge and the nephews coming up the walk, everyone hid.

Uncle Scrooge opened the door. "If it weren't for those kids, I would've caught a fish," he grumbled.

"Surprise!" yelled all the guests.

"Happy birthday, Uncle Scrooge!" shouted Huey, Dewey, and Louie.

Uncle Scrooge smiled. "I thought you all forgot," he said. And he hugged his nephews as everyone sang "Happy Birthday."

A Visit to Grandma Duck's Farm

Huey, Dewey, and Louie couldn't wait to get to Grandma Duck's farm.
"I'm going to go horseback riding," said Huey.

"The first thing I'm going to do is jump in the pond," said Dewey.

When they got to the farm, Grandma Duck was waiting for them on
the porch. "Good morning, boys," she said. "Come inside and have
breakfast. I have something to tell you."

The boys sat down to a big breakfast. "Jake, our hired hand, isn't
feeling well," said Grandma. "The work around here is really piling up."

"We'll do it!" said the boys.

"Well, there's quite a bit of work to do," said Grandma. "The pigsty and the stables have to be cleaned, the cows need milking, the eggs have to be gathered, and the hay needs stacking. Do you think you can handle all of that?" asked Grandma.

"No problem!" said Louie.

"While you're out working up an appetite I'll be in the kitchen, cooking up a storm," Grandma said. "At least you'll have something to look forward to after working so hard."

"You won't have to call us twice!" said Huey.

"This is a lot harder than it looks!" said Dewey as he milked what seemed like the hundredth cow.

"It sure is," agreed Louie. "But just keep your mind on dinner. Do you think Grandma will bake one of her pies?"

"Sure," said Huey. "Maybe even two of them!"

Then they went to do the rest of the chores. The boys worked harder than they ever had before. Soon all they had left to do was stack the hay.

"I can't wait to have some of Grandma's mashed potatoes and gravy," said Louie, his mouth watering.

"And don't forget her homemade biscuits!" added Dewey.

"Let's hurry up and finish!" Huey said.

Meanwhile, Grandma Duck was putting the finishing touches on her dinner. She called out the window to the three boys. "Where can they be?" she thought.

She looked for them in the henhouse. She looked in the dairy barn. She looked in the pigsty and in the stables. When Grandma got to the hayfield, she heard some strange noises.

"Just as I thought," she said to herself. There, sound asleep and snoring loudly, were the three boys.

"It looks like those little guys have tired themselves out," Grandma said. "But it would be a shame for them to miss dinner."

Grandma shook the boys gently. "Come on, boys," she said, "it's time for dinner."

Huey sat up and rubbed the sleep from his eyes. "I guess you did have to call us twice, Grandma," he said. And they headed off to eat a delicious meal.

Bambi to the Rescue

One spring morning Bambi was frolicking through the forest when he heard a strange sound. He followed the sound until he came to some bushes. Hidden among a pile of leaves was a little baby animal sobbing.

"Please don't cry," said Bambi. "My name is Bambi. What's yours?"

"P-P-Peggy," said the baby. "I'm lost. I was riding on my mother's tail with my brothers and sisters. And then I fell off!" she wailed.

"Don't you worry," said Bambi. "I'll help you find your mother." He bent his long legs and knelt very close to Peggy.

"Climb aboard," Bambi said. Peggy crawled onto Bambi's back and held on to his neck very tightly.

Their first stop was at the home of Mrs. Rabbit. Bambi stuck his nose in the opening that led to the underground home.

"Mrs. Rabbit," Bambi called, "did you lose one of your babies?"

"Certainly not!" she answered. "I've got them all right here."

"Thanks, anyway," said Bambi.

The next stop was Mrs. Squirrel's house. "Mrs. Squirrel," Bambi called up to the tree, "are you missing one of your babies?"

"Not at the moment, Bambi," Mrs. Squirrel said. "They're all playing in this tree."

Bambi decided to try Mrs. Groundhog next. He stomped on the ground near the mound that led to her underground tunnel.

Mrs. Groundhog poked her nose up through the mound. Two very sleepy eyes stared out at Bambi.

"I'm sorry to disturb your sleep, Mrs. Groundhog," said Bambi, "but I found a new baby and I wondered if she was yours."

"I don't think so," said Mrs. Groundhog, yawning. "You see, I haven't had my babies yet this year."

Bambi and Peggy went to see Mrs. Chipmunk. Bambi knocked on the tree above the hole that led to the chipmunk's home.

Mrs. Chipmunk came scurrying out. "Good morning, Bambi," she said. "What can I do for you?"

"Is there any chance this baby belongs to you?" Bambi asked.

"She couldn't possibly," said Mrs. Chipmunk. "Chipmunks don't have opossum babies. Why don't you try Mrs. Opossum's tree over there."

Bambi trotted over to the next tree. Before he could say anything, Mrs. Opossum called from high above, "Peggy!"

"Mommy!" cried Peggy. "We've been looking all over for you!"

"I've been looking for you, too, dear," said Mrs. Opossum. "Thank you for bringing her home, Bambi."

Peggy looked at her new friend. "Can I have a ride again sometime?" she asked Bambi.

"Anytime, Peggy," Bambi answered.